For Ivy —E.J.

To Monika —T.B.

Text copyright © 2004 by Emily Jenkins
Pictures copyright © 2004 by Tomek Bogacki
All rights reserved
Distributed in Canada by Douglas & McIntyre Ltd.
Color separations by Chroma Graphics PTE Ltd.
Printed and bound in the United States of America by Phoenix Color Corporation
Designed by Barbara Grzeslo
First edition, 2004
10 9 8 7 6 5 4 3 2 1

Library of Congress Cataloging-in-Publication Data
Jenkins, Emily.
    Daffodil / Emily Jenkins ; pictures by Tomek Bogacki.— 1st ed.
      p. cm.
    Summary: Triplet sisters Rose, Violet, and Daffodil grow tired of wearing the
colorful party dresses that match their names.
    ISBN 0-374-31676-7
    [1. Individuality—Fiction.   2. Clothing and dress—Fiction.   3. Triplets—
Fiction.   4. Sisters—Fiction.]   I. Bogacki, Tomasz, ill.   II. Title.

PZ7.J4134 Daf 2004
[E]—dc21
                               2002026509

Daffodil

Emily Jenkins

Pictures by Tomek Bogacki

Frances Foster Books
Farrar, Straus and Giroux
New York

Daffodil had two sisters,
and they all three looked alike.
People couldn't tell them apart.
Not even Mommy, sometimes.

But Daffodil always could.
And Violet and Rose
could, too.

Violet had a squinty
look in her eyes that
made her seem like
she was thinking.

Rose had a dimple in her chin.

And Daffodil had a big mouth.

Daffodil's mommy
liked to go to parties,
and when she did,
she put her children
in fancy party dresses
of different colors.
"That way," she said,
"everyone can tell
who is who, and
which is which."

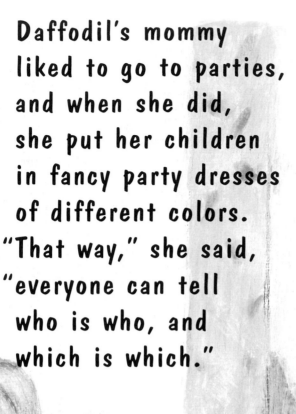

Violet's dress was violet,
with lots of lace. It was
very, very pretty.

Rose's dress was
pink, with little
bows all over.

It was

even

prettier.

Lucky

ducks.

But Daffodil's dress was
yellow. Sour, fake-cheerful
yellow that reminded
Daffodil of pee.
It had weird fake pearls
on the bottom.

Daffodil hated that yellow dress

very

extremely

hugely

much.

At the parties, Violet used to twirl in her pretty violet dress. People would notice her and say, "You must be Violet." They'd usually give her some petits fours or a piece of cake.

Rose would twirl in her pretty
pink dress, and people would say,
"You must be Rose."
Maybe they'd give her some
hard candy.

Daffodil never felt like twirling in that pee-yellow dress. Instead, she'd sit in the biggest armchair she could find and make a sour face. Then people would come over and say, in fake-cheerful voices . . .

"Let me see, you must be **Sunflower.**

Or is it **Forsythia?**"

"How about **Marigold?**"

"**Buttercup?**"

"**Mustard?**"

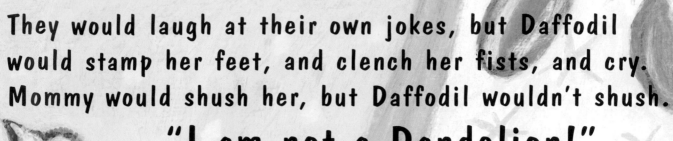

They would laugh at their own jokes, but Daffodil would stamp her feet, and clench her fists, and cry. Mommy would shush her, but Daffodil wouldn't shush.

"I am not a Dandelion!"

she'd scream,

and end up in the
bathroom all alone—
not being offered anything
special to eat at all.
Why couldn't she wear pink,
like Rose?
Or violet,
like Violet?

Such

lucky

ducks.

One day, when they were all
getting ready for a party,
enough was enough.

Very
extremely
hugely
much,
enough.

"I hate it,
I hate it,
I hate it!"
yelled Daffodil.

Then and there,
she refused to wear
the yellow dress.

Not now,
not
ever
again.

Mommy looked confused.
Rose looked surprised.

But that lucky
duck Violet burst
into tears.

"Why can't I wear yellow,
like Daffodil?" she cried.
"Or pink, like Rose?
They always get the
pretty colors."

"You can have it, then!"
yelled Rose, all of a sudden—
throwing her dress on the floor.

"I don't want it. I hate pink!

In fact,
I hate it
very
extremely

hugely
much."

Mommy said she was sorry. And from that day on, Violet, Rose, and Daffodil traded dresses whenever they felt like it. Nobody at the parties could tell who was who, or which was which.

But Daffodil could. And Violet and Rose could, too. And so could Mommy (most of the time).

One day, not long after, they grew out of those dresses. Mommy let them choose new party clothes in any colors they wanted.

Violet picked black, with a pleated skirt.

Rose picked plaid,
with a velvet sash.

And Daffodil,

she got cherry red pants with a matching jacket.
They all felt

very

lucky

ducky

indeed.